P9-AOG-711

A PIG, A FOX, AND A FOX

For teachers, past and present,
with gratefulness and admiration—JF

PENGUIN WORKSHOP
An Imprint of Penguin Random House LLC, New York

Penguin supports copyright. Copyright fuels creativity, encourages diverse voices, promotes free speech, and creates a vibrant culture. Thank you for buying an authorized edition of this book and for complying with copyright laws by not reproducing, scanning, or distributing any part of it in any form without permission. You are supporting writers and allowing Penguin to continue to publish books for every reader.

Copyright © 2020 by Jonathan Fenske. All rights reserved. Published by Penguin Workshop, an imprint of Penguin Random House LLC, New York. PENGUIN and PENGUIN WORKSHOP are trademarks of Penguin Books Ltd, and the W colophon is a registered trademark of Penguin Random House LLC. Manufactured in China.

Visit us online at www.penguinrandomhouse.com.

Library of Congress Cataloging-in-Publication Data is available.

ISBN 9781524792121 (paperback) 10 9 8 7 6 5 4 3 2 1
ISBN 9780593382561 (library binding) 10 9 8 7 6 5 4 3 2 1

A PIG, A FOX, AND A FOX

by Jonathan Fenske

Penguin Workshop

PART ONE

I am little.
I am big.
I have a doll named Mister Fox!
I keep him in my trusty box.

I look like him.
He looks like me.
A perfect match!
Do you agree?

We like to hide.
We like to play.
Two foxes will
trick Pig today.

I take some blocks.
I build a wall.
I build it big.
I build it tall.

I climb up high with Mister Fox.
I set him on the wall of blocks.

Hey, Pig!
Look up!
Look up and see
a Fox on top of blocks.
Yippee!

I look around.
Where is that Fox?
?

I see a wall.
A wall of blocks.
Tee-hee.

I see Fox sitting on the wall!
If those blocks tip, that Fox will fall!

Oh, this is bad!
Oh, Fox! Beware!
You should not
play around up there!

Please do not move.
Please do not jump.
TRIP!
CRASH!
Oh no!
I gave the
blocks a bump.
GULP.

I bumped the wall.
The wall of blocks.
The wall will fall!
And so will Fox!
I will catch you!
Do not fear!
Your good friend Pig
is always here!

PLOP!

You silly Pig! That was a doll.
That was not Fox up on the wall!
saved a doll.
I bumped some blocks.
I smashed a wall.

And smooshed a Fox.

PART TWO

He is little.
He is big.
I have a doll.
I have a box.
I love to play
with Mister Fox!

Pig has a house.

Pig has a door.

I knock and knock.

KNOCK! KNOCK!

KNOCK!

I knock some more.

One Fox will hide.
One Fox will stay.

Two foxes will
trick Pig today.

Is that my friend? Yahoo! Hooray! My friend the Fox has come to play!

Unlock the door and swing it wide!
I always let my friends inside!
CRACK!
Ouch.
SWEET
You are not Fox! No. Not at all.

Groan.
You are not Fox.
You are his doll.

Oh, silly me.
That sneaky Fox
has tricked me with
his sneaky knocks.

That sneaky Fox. He is so bad!
That sneaky Fox. He makes me mad!

I heard some knocks.

I turned the locks.

I broke a door.

And broke a Fox.
SWEET
STY

PART THREE

I am little.
I am big.
We like to hide.
We like to play.

But we have had enough today.

I say goodbye to Mister Fox.
And put him back into his box.

DISCARDED

J EASY FENSKE
Fenske, Jonathan,
A pig, a fox, and a fox /
R2005728551 PTREE

Atlanta-Fulton Public Library